[WITHDRAWN FROM STOCK]
LIBRARIES NI

Oliver Moon's Christmas Cracker

Sue Mongredien

Illustrated by

Jan McCafferty

USBORNE

D0495636

WESTERN EDUCATION AND LIBRARY BOARD	
C502846610	
Bertrams	17.11.07
J	£3.99

LIBRARIES NI
WITHDRAWN FROM STOCK

For Joshua and Rachel Thulborn, with lots of love

First published in 2007 by Usborne Publishing Ltd., Usborne House, 83-85 Saffron Hill, London EC1N 8RT, England. www.usborne.com

Text copyright © Sue Mongredien, 2007

Illustration copyright © Usborne Publishing Ltd., 2007

The right of Sue Mongredien to be identified as the author of this work has been asserted by her in accordance with the Copyright, Designs and Patents Act, 1988.

The name Usborne and the devices ♀ ⊕ are Trade Marks of Usborne Publishing Ltd.

All rights reserved. No part of this publication may be reproduced, stored in a retrieval system or transmitted in any form or by any means, electronic, mechanical, photocopying, recording or otherwise without the prior permission of the publisher.

This is a work of fiction. The characters, incidents, and dialogues are products of the author's imagination and are not to be construed as real. Any resemblance to actual events or persons, living or dead, is entirely coincidental.

A CIP catalogue record for this book is available from the British Library.

JFM MJJASOND/07   ISBN 9780746077931

Printed in Great Britain.

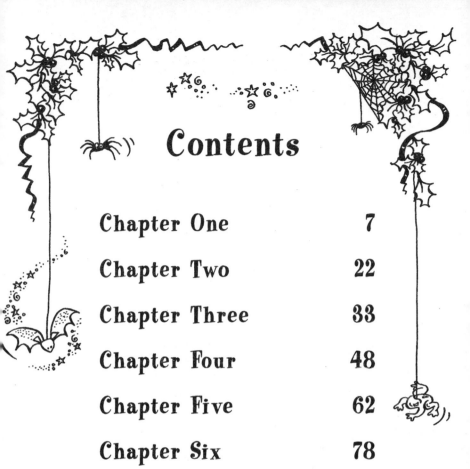

Contents

Chapter
One

Oliver Moon opened his eyes, yawned sleepily and stretched. Then an exciting thought struck him, and he sat bolt upright, wide awake all of a sudden.

It was the first day of the Christmas holidays, and Magic School was closed for two whole weeks! Even better, the weather wizards had predicted a white

Christmas. Oliver really hoped it would snow soon. He and his best friend, Jake Frogfreckle, were dying to go sledging down Cacklewick Hill together, not to mention have a few good snowball fights, too!

Oliver grabbed his wand from the bedside table and pointed it at his bedroom window. "Curtain, open!" he commanded.

The end of his wand made a crackling noise…but nothing happened.

Oliver waited a moment, then sighed impatiently and blew on it to warm it up. His wand was very temperamental in the cold. He gave it a little shake, then tried again. "Is there snow? Curtain – go!" he ordered.

His wand crackled a bit louder, and a few golden sparks fizzled at its tip, but the curtain stayed firmly shut. Oliver swung his legs out of his spiderweb hammock and ran to open the curtain himself...only to see the back garden as green and wild as ever, without a single snowflake in sight.

Oliver stared up at the sky, hoping to see a few snow clouds on the horizon. No such luck. The sun was shining, and a crow was cawing cheerfully in the tanglebranch tree. It looked more like spring than winter!

Pulling on his dressing gown, Oliver headed downstairs for breakfast. Never mind. It was only the twentieth of December today, so there was plenty of time for snow. And in the meantime there were all sorts of other fun things to do before Christmas Day – decorating the Prickletree, making paper chains, and, of course, helping his parents cook lots of yummy Christmas food... Mmm! Minced eyes! His favourite!

"Morning, Oliver," his dad said, as

Oliver entered the kitchen. "Would you like some frogspawn porridge for breakfast?"

"Yes, please," Oliver said, sitting down at the table next to his little sister, the Witch Baby.

"Nice," she told him, with a loud burp.

Mrs. Moon, Oliver's mum, was opening Christmas cards at the table. "Here's one from the Banshees," she said, reading the note inside. "Oh, look, and they've sent a hologram of little Ethelbert with his first junior wand. Isn't he sweet?"

She held up the card and, inside, Oliver saw a sparkling picture of a tufty-haired toddler brandishing a purple wand.

"And this one's from the Batbottoms, and here's one from the Toadtrumpers," Mrs. Moon went on, passing them over so that Oliver and his dad could read them. Then she ran a long green fingernail under the seal of the last envelope to open it. She drew out a glossy card with a photo on the front. "Oh, and here's one from Wart and Merv," she said, gazing at the photo. "Gosh, haven't Thug and Thugette grown!"

Oliver leaned over to have a closer look at his mum's sister, his Aunt Wart. She was posing with her husband, Oliver's Uncle Merv, in the grounds of their mansion house. Oliver's cousins, Thug and Thugette, stood in front of their parents, both sneering sulkily into the camera.

"Grown ugly, you mean," Oliver muttered under his breath, taking in Thug's mop of greasy hair and Thugette's single bushy eyebrow. He didn't like his cousins much. The last time he'd seen them, they'd tried to lock him in the family's haunted cellar. And then, once he'd escaped, they'd dropped a load of itch-beetles down his cloak.

Just then the photo started shimmering,

and a pink vapour spiralled up from
the card.

"Oh, they've added a
Magic Message," said
Mr. Moon, raising
his eyebrows.
"Very posh."

The Moons
watched as the pink
vapour formed into
the shape of a sprite,
hovering above the table.

"Message from Wart," it announced.
"Inviting you all to come for Christmas
in Toadstool Towers."

Mr. Moon pulled a face, and then,
realizing Oliver was watching him
curiously, forced a smile. "What a shame,

we're busy this year," he told the sprite. "Never mind."

The sprite cocked an eyebrow. "Busy? Let's see…" It darted towards the wall where the family calendar hung. The sprite tapped the calendar cheekily. "No, you're not! There's nothing written on here!"

He zipped back to the table. "She's expecting you, anyway. Dinner tonight. Don't be late!"

"But—" Mr. Moon protested.

Whoosh! Before he could utter another word, the sprite had vanished with a burst of pink sparkles.

"Gone!" the Witch Baby said, her eyes round with amazement. "All gone!"

"Yes, just like our plans for Christmas," Mr. Moon muttered. He sat down heavily and leaned across the table towards Oliver's mum. "You know, I was really looking forward to spending Christmas at home, dear."

"Me, too," Oliver put in. He gazed beseechingly at his mum. "Couldn't we phone her, and say we're not coming after all?"

Mrs. Moon glanced down at the card. "You heard what the sprite said – they're expecting us today." She gave a bright smile. "I'm sure we'll have a lovely time there. We can always come home for New Year, can't we?"

Oliver stared at her in dismay. "You mean we're going?" he asked.

She nodded. "We're going," she replied.

"But what about the Prickletree?" Oliver protested. Decorating the tree was one of his favourite Christmas traditions. On the first day of December every year, Oliver's family, and wizards and witches all over the world, planted a Prickleseed in a pot, then worked some special Christmas magic. Over the next few weeks, the Prickletree grew bigger and spikier by the day, dripping with glossy purple berries and dark green thorns.

Then, on the last day of
December, it vanished,
leaving one single
purple seed for
the following
Christmas.

The Moons'
Prickletree was
huge this year.
It had sprawled
almost up to the
ceiling in the
living room,
and Oliver
had really been
looking forward
to decorating it.
His mum and

dad kept a big box of
decorations in the
attic – little sparkly
bats and glass frogs
and glittery
spiders, all on
gold threads. On
Christmas Eve, Mr. Moon
always brought down the
box so that Oliver could hang the
trinkets from the tree's spikes.

"We can decorate it when we get back,"
Mrs. Moon told him.

"That won't be the same," Oliver said.
He stared out of the window, feeling as if
he'd been robbed of his Christmas before
it had even begun. "And what about
sledging with Jake?"

"When we get back," his mum repeated. "We'll have a cracking Christmas holiday, Oliver. You'll see."

Oliver pushed his frogspawn porridge away, not feeling hungry any more. Whatever his mum said, he knew already that Christmas at Aunt Wart's house wasn't going to be any fun at all!

Chapter Two

The Moons' house was a flurry of activity
for the whole morning. Mrs. Moon
packed clothes for everyone, and Mr.
Moon recharged the broomsticks with
flying magic. Oliver wrapped the
presents he'd chosen for his family, while
the Witch Baby spent the entire time
trying to climb the Prickletree, and

crying every time she was jabbed by one
of the spikes.

The lizardphone squeaked mid-
morning. It was Jake. "Brilliant news!"
he cried. "Mum's got us tickets for the
pantomime tomorrow — and she's bought
one for you too!"

Oliver groaned. Oh, no! He'd been dying to see *Witcherella*, this year's pantomime, at the Cacklewick Theatre. But now...

"I won't be able to go," he replied miserably. "We're flying to my aunt's this afternoon, 'cos we're spending Christmas with them now."

"Oh!" Jake said, sounding surprised. "I didn't know you were going away."

"Neither did I, until breakfast time," Oliver said. His shoulders slumped as he caught sight of Aunt Wart's card on the mantelpiece. How he wished his mum hadn't opened it in the first place! "I guess you'll have to ask someone else to go with you."

"Yeah," said Jake. He sounded almost as disappointed as Oliver. "Well…happy Christmas, then, Oliver."

"Happy Christmas, Jake. Enjoy *Witcherella*."

Oliver clicked the lizardphone back on its stand and glared at a framed photo of Aunt Wart's family on the wall. "This is all *your* fault!" he muttered to the picture. "You and your stupid Magic Message!"

*

After lunch, Mrs. Moon magicked their suitcases off to Aunt Wart's house, and Mr. Moon strapped the Witch Baby into her broomstick baby seat. "Let's go," he said. "Oliver, stay close to me while we're flying. It's a long way."

"Okay, Dad," Oliver said, gripping his broomstick handle. He gave a last look at his house, then the whole family took off into the cold, clear sky, their cloaks swirling out behind them.

A bottom-numbing four hours later, Oliver's parents nosed their broomsticks downward, and landed in the grounds of a huge, stone manor house. Oliver steered after them, glad to have arrived at last.

Mr. Moon unstrapped the Witch Baby, who had fallen fast asleep, her black woolly bonnet slipping over her eyes. "Right," he said, "I suppose we'd better—"

"There you are!" came a plummy voice. "Coo-ee!"

Oliver looked around to see his aunt waddling down the garden path, waving. Uncle Merv followed behind her, the winter sunlight glinting off his bald patch.

Mrs. Moon smiled and hurried towards her sister, her broomstick under her arm.

"Wart! Hello! So kind of you to invite us over," she said.

"Our pleasure, Deirdre, our pleasure!" Aunt Wart replied, hugging Oliver's mum. Oliver saw his aunt frown as her hand brushed against Mrs. Moon's broomstick. "What the…? Oh, a broomstick! Heavens, Deirdre, do you still fly around on such an old-fashioned contraption?"

Mrs. Moon's cheeks turned pink. "Well, yes," she replied, holding it protectively. "Don't you?"

"Not likely," barked Uncle Merv, who had the bushiest eyebrows Oliver had ever seen. "Didn't Wart tell you? We've got our own Spellicopter these days. Flies like a dream, does the old chopper!" He cast a disdainful look at the Moon family's broomsticks. "Gosh, they're very grubby, aren't they?" he said, wrinkling his large nose. "Better leave them out here, eh? Don't want them making a mess of the house!"

"No, of course not," Mr. Moon said tightly. He passed the sleeping Witch Baby to Mrs. Moon, then gathered all the broomsticks together and stacked them up by a nearby shed. Then he took a deep breath and stuck out his hand to Uncle Merv. "Nice to see you again, Merv. Business going well?"

Uncle Merv squared his shoulders. "Very well, old boy," he said. "Turnover up five hundred per cent this year. We're as rich as royalty these days!"

He slapped Mr. Moon on the back, and gave a loud booming laugh, which woke the Witch Baby.

Oliver's sister stirred in Mrs. Moon's arms, then gazed around with sleepy, pink-rimmed eyes. She caught sight of Aunt Wart and Uncle Merv, and promptly burst into loud tears.

Oliver knew just how she felt.

Chapter Three

"Your luggage arrived a little while ago," Aunt Wart told them. "Thug and Thugette have taken it to your rooms for you." She winced as the Witch Baby's yells reached a higher pitch. "Can't you do something to *stop* her?"

"Probably not," Mr. Moon replied truthfully.

Then Aunt Wart spotted Oliver, and loomed towards him. "Oliver!" she shrilled. "Come and give your aunty a kiss!"

Oliver shut his eyes hurriedly as her great lipsticked mouth neared his. Her glasses pressed into the side of his face as her wet lips landed on his cheek.

"*Mwah!* Just look at you," she said, finally drawing back. "Quite the little wizard, aren't you?"

Oliver smiled politely, but was too grossed-out by the kiss to speak. Ugh! Why did his aunt *always* have to do that?

"Thug and Thugette are *dying* to see you, Oliver. They insisted on decorating your room for you," she went on. She straightened her pointy hat and smiled. "Now, then. Come this way, and I'll show you where you're all sleeping."

She and Uncle Merv strode up the garden path and into the house, their midnight-black cloaks swishing behind them. Oliver and his family followed behind, the Witch Baby still snivelling into Mrs. Moon's shoulder.

"There, there," Mrs. Moon said comfortingly, patting the Witch Baby's little back. "Everything's all right. Everything's all right."

Oliver couldn't help rolling his eyes. Everything all right? As if!

"And here's *your* room, Oliver," Aunt Wart said. She was showing them around the house, which, in Oliver's opinion, was taking a long time. His parents had already had to *ooh* and *ahh* politely over the new kitchen extension, the Spellipad and Spellicopter, the new master bedroom, complete with en-suite mud bath and waterfall…

"Only the best for me and my folks," Uncle Merv kept saying. "Only the very best!"

Oliver pushed open the door of the room Aunt Wart had said was his, and…

"Boo!"

"BOO!"

Two terrifying-looking ogres jumped out at him.

Oliver gasped, and the Witch Baby started wailing all over again.

"Oh, you two," Aunt Wart chided. "Thug, Thugette, take off those horrible masks and say hello."

Thug removed his ogre mask. He wasn't much better looking in real life. "All right?" he muttered, his eyes sliding away from Oliver.

Thugette pushed her mask up on top of her long, straggly hair. "Hi there," she simpered. "We've just been making your room look nice, Oliver."

"How kind!" Aunt Wart beamed. "What angels you are, both of you."

Oliver stared past his aunt to see that

his cousins had put branches of holly on his pillow – very funny – and had hung up pictures of grinning skeletons and werewolves, with blood dripping from their mouths. Oliver's suitcase lay open on the bed, his clothes scattered everywhere, and Oliver prickled with annoyance. He hated the thought of his cousins going through his stuff. It looked as if they'd been nosing through his Christmas presents, too. What a cheek!

Oliver stepped into the room and Thug promptly tripped him up. "Ow," Oliver muttered, rubbing his funny bone where he'd bashed it against the wardrobe. He glared at Thug, hoping someone would tell him off, but Uncle Merv was waffling on to Mr. Moon about the loft conversion

they were planning, and Aunt Wart was
busy talking to Oliver's mum.

"Now, I'll let you get ready for dinner,"
she was saying, "while I rustle something
up in the kitchen. We'll eat at six, okay?"

"Lovely," Mrs. Moon said. "I'll come

and help. Oliver, play nicely with your cousins, won't you?"

Oliver scowled as the door shut behind them, and he was left alone with Thug and Thugette.

Thug went across to Oliver's suitcase. "These for us?" he asked, holding up the presents Oliver had wrapped for his family.

"So kind of you, Ollie," Thugette smirked, leaning against the wall.

"They're not for *you*," Oliver said, snatching the presents away from Thug. "They're for my mum and dad and sister."

"What have you got 'em?" Thug asked nosily, sitting on the bed and putting his smelly feet on Oliver's suitcase.

"A hairy spider for my sister, a photo of our family in a picture frame I painted for my dad, and I made my mum a candlestick at school," Oliver said. "How about you?"

"I've got Mum a new witch-watch," Thug drawled, "and Dad some pilot goggles for the Spellicopter."

"And I've got them a brand new wand

each," Thugette said smugly, "with solid silver wand-holders. Top of the range, they are."

"Wow," Oliver said. He couldn't help feeling that his presents were going to look a bit…well, *cheap* next to his cousins' lavish gifts.

"The only thing is," Thug said, leaning forward, "Mum's already gone and got herself a new watch, just the other day. So I was wondering… Would you like to swap presents? You could give *your* mum the witch-watch, and I could give *mine* the candlestick. My mum loves all that home-made rubbish, you see."

Oliver frowned. "What's the catch?" he asked. This sounded too good to be true.

Thug held up his hands, as if surprised

by Oliver's question. "Catch? There's no catch," he said. "I'll show you the watch if you like." He rummaged in his cloak pocket and drew out an elegant gold box. He snapped it open to reveal a wristwatch on a slim bangle, with diamonds studded around the clock face.

"Wow," Oliver said again. "And you really want to swap this for my candlestick?" He could hardly believe his cousin was being so generous.

"Sure," Thug said breezily. "So…what do you say?"

Oliver imagined his mum opening her present on Christmas morning and finding the witch-watch. She didn't have any fancy jewellery at all. He could just picture her eyes lighting up as she saw it, and tried it on her wrist. "Well, if you're certain?" he said, checking Thug's face.

Thug nodded, a sweaty hand already on the wrapped candlestick. "I'm certain," he replied.

"Then…thanks," Oliver said, closing the gold box carefully. "Thanks a lot, Thug."

"No probs," Thug said. "Catch ya later, Ollie."

Thugette winked at him as she and her brother left the room, and Oliver sat staring at the golden box in his hand. Then he grinned to himself. Maybe it was going to be a merry Christmas, after all. His mum was certainly going to be one happy witch on Christmas Day, that was for sure!

Chapter
Four

Despite Oliver's burst of optimism, the
next few days weren't much fun at all.
Thug and Thugette had a whole range of
tricks up their cloak sleeves, and seemed
determined to try them all out on Oliver.
First there was the poisonous snake in his
pyjamas. Then there was the push into
the frog-pond. And then, when the two

families went out on a day trip to a
monster maze, they cast a Fly-away spell
on Oliver, to try and get him lost.

Luckily for Oliver, the spell wasn't
strong enough to whizz him away too far
– but it did send him flying straight into
a large thornspike tree, which was
extremely painful.

"Bad Thug. Nasty Thugette," the
Witch Baby said sympathetically,
as she watched Mrs. Moon pulling the
thorns out.

"I'm sure it was an accident," Mrs.
Moon said, not meeting Oliver's eye.

Finally it was Christmas Day. Surely his rotten cousins would lay off him today? Oliver thought blearily as he rolled over in bed. Then, as he opened his eyes, he realized that something was different. A dazzling white light was shining through the crack in the curtains and it took him a moment to work out what had happened. Had it really...? Had it actually snowed?

He jumped out of bed and raced to the window, pulling the curtains wide open. He blinked at the brightness – and then grinned at the great expanse of white that lay outside. Snow. Snow, everywhere!

Oliver felt a pang of homesickness as he wondered if it had snowed back in Cacklewick. He couldn't help imagining what fun he'd be having with Jake right now, if only the Moons were home…

Thick flakes of white were still tumbling down through the air. "Too much of a blizzard for anyone to go out in it yet," Uncle Merv ruled over breakfast. "At this rate, we're going to

be snowed in – won't that be jolly?"

Oliver looked down at his plate of hog slices and ostrich eggs. *Wouldn't it be jolly awful, more like,* he thought. Snowed in, with his horrible cousins – he couldn't think of anything worse!

After breakfast, the two families sat down together in the living room to exchange presents. The Witch Baby was delighted by her pet spider, kissing it all over its hairy little face, until it was quite damp. "Mine," she told it proudly. "All mine!"

Oliver's dad seemed to really like the photo frame Oliver had painted, too. "I shall keep it on my desk at work," he said, hugging Oliver warmly. "Thanks, son!"

Meanwhile, Aunt Wart was unwrapping the candlestick. "I made it myself," Thug boasted, with a sly wink at Oliver.

"Oh! Did you hear that everyone? My little Thuggy made this for me!" Aunt Wart exclaimed, holding up

the candlestick so everyone could see. "Isn't it beautiful?"

"It's lovely," Oliver's mum said. "Well done, Thug. You must have spent ages on it!"

"Here's my present to you," Oliver said, handing his mum the gold box. "Happy Christmas, Mum." Then he held his breath as she opened it.

"Oh, Oliver!" she cried, her eyes as bright as stars. She looked completely stunned, Oliver thought to himself happily. "A witch-watch...for me? It's...it's absolutely gorgeous!"

Mr. Moon's eyebrows shot up as he saw it. "Where did you get the money for that?" he asked Oliver, staring at the watch as if he couldn't believe his eyes.

"It looks like it cost a bomb!"

Oliver tapped his nose secretively. "Can't say," he replied. He smiled at the look of joy on his mum's face as she tried on the watch, and admired it on her wrist. She loved it. What a result!

He grinned across at Thug. He was
really pleased he'd swapped presents with
his cousin now. The watch was far and
away the nicest thing he'd ever given
his mum.

Just then, there was a loud knock at
the front door. Aunt Wart
frowned, and pushed
up her glasses.
"Who could that
be, I wonder,
coming round
on Christmas
morning?" she
muttered. "Back in a minute, everyone!"
"Here's your present from me and your
dad," Oliver's mum said as Aunt Wart
left the room. "Happy Christmas, love."

Oliver ripped open the paper eagerly – and cheered. A wand-warmer! Just what he needed for cold days. "Thanks, Mum. Thanks, Dad," he said  happily. "This is perfect! Just what I..."

Oliver fell silent as he heard an angry shout from outside the room, and looked around curiously.

"Well, I'm telling you, it was stolen from right under our Prickletree!" a man was yelling. "And I'd like to see if anyone here knows anything about it!"

The door burst open, and a furious

looking wizard appeared with snowflakes
in his beard. He glared at everyone, his
hands on his hips.

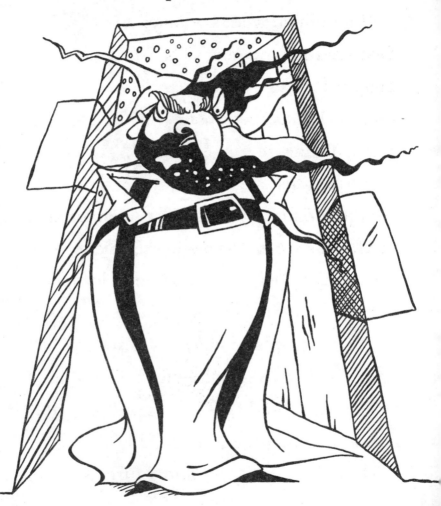

"Happy Christmas, Mr. Doorcreak," Uncle Merv said in surprise. "What's wrong?"

"I'll tell you what's wrong," Mr. Doorcreak thundered. "The watch I bought for my wife has been stolen and—" He stopped shouting, his eyes narrowing as he saw Mrs. Moon's Christmas watch glinting on her wrist. "And there it is!" he bellowed. He glared at Oliver's mum. "So *you're* the thief, are you?"

Chapter
Five

There was a shocked silence. "I certainly
am not!" Mrs. Moon said indignantly.
"This watch was a present to me, thank
you very much."

Oliver's stomach lurched as the truth
hit him. The watch was stolen? So Thug
must have tricked him! Thug hadn't
bought the watch at all. He had pinched

it, then set the whole thing up so that now it looked as if *Oliver* was the thief!

"A present?" Mr. Doorcreak snapped, striding over to her. "From whom?"

Oliver's mouth was horribly dry. "From me," he managed to say. "But——"

Aunt Wart sucked in her breath, and exchanged a knowing glance with her husband. "Oliver Moon, I can't believe it," she exclaimed. "I know your family aren't exactly rolling in it, but to go stealing…!"

"But I didn't——" Oliver began.

"Oliver's never stolen anything in his life," Mr. Moon said, rounding on Aunt Wart. "I'm sure there's a perfectly reasonable——"

"Where did you get it from, Ollie?" his

mum asked. The sparkle had left her eyes now, and she bit her lip anxiously as she waited for his response.

"From *him*," Oliver said, pointing at Thug. "And *I* made that candlestick for *you*, Mum. Only Thug said he wanted to swap presents, and—"

"I don't know what he's talking about," Thug said, his eyes wide.

"Don't try and get my son into trouble," Aunt Wart shrieked. "He's done nothing wrong!"

Mrs. Moon took the watch off her wrist and put it back in the gold box.

"I didn't steal it, Mum," Oliver said. "I promise you I didn't!"

"Well, somebody did," Mr. Doorcreak said, lowering his dark bushy eyebrows in disapproval. "Thank you," he said, as Mrs. Moon handed him the box.

He left the room, and a terrible silence fell.

"I didn't steal the watch," Oliver said again, feeling as if he might cry. How could he have been so stupid as to fall for Thug's trick? "I didn't!"

Aunt Wart gave a disbelieving snort, and Oliver dropped his gaze. She didn't believe him. Did *anyone* believe him?

The Witch Baby crawled over and put her arm around him. "Good Ollie," she said defensively. "Good boy."

Oliver had a lump in his throat as he turned to his parents. His dad forced a smile, but his mum had a dreadful sadness about her face. A disappointed kind of look. It made Oliver feel sick inside, like he'd let her down.

"Where were we? Oh yes. Here's a present for you, Merv," Oliver's dad said, trying to sound jolly, as if the whole watch incident hadn't just happened.

"Thank you," Uncle Merv said. He
looked at the present as if he might catch
something nasty from it.

"Thug, Thugette, something very
special for you two, for being so *good* all
year," Aunt Wart said pointedly,
handing over two enormous presents
to them.

Oliver turned away, not wanting to see. His eyes fell upon the candlestick he'd made and he felt a wrench inside. Now his mum had *nothing* from him.

I haven't done anything wrong! he reminded himself. *All I wanted was to give my mum a really nice present. And now I feel like a criminal!* He gave a heavy sigh. There was only one thing for it. He had to prove that it was Thug who stole the watch...but how?

Over lunch, Aunt Wart handed around a box of Christmas crackers. "There should be some good prizes in these," she boasted. "They were *extremely* expensive!" She pounced on a pink one, her greedy little eyes glittering. "Ahh – I think I know what's in here. I'll have this one," she grinned.

She pulled the pink cracker with Uncle Merv and seemed disappointed when a silver dragon toy fell out. "The baby had better have this," she said, tossing it over with a sigh.

Mr. and Mrs. Moon pulled their crackers next. Mr. Moon found a mini Stardust-sucker in his. "Collect unlimited stardust at the flick of a switch, as you fly on your broomstick!" he read aloud. He raised his eyebrows. "Very nifty."

Mrs. Moon had a walkie-talkie set in her cracker. "You have it," she said, passing it to Oliver. "I bet you and Jake could have some fun with this!"

"Thanks, Mum," Oliver said. He held his own cracker out to the Witch Baby. "Want to pull this with me?"

"BANG!" the Witch Baby shouted as the cracker's snap went off. Oliver gave her the purple party hat to wear, and he gobbled up the Brilliant Ideas sweet inside. "Eat this – guaranteed to give you at least three brilliant ideas!" it said on the wrapper.

Then he gasped at the other present that had fallen out of the cracker. A black pearl bracelet – just the thing for his mum!

"That's the present *I* wanted!" Aunt Wart pouted, spotting it too, but Oliver pretended he hadn't heard her.

"Here, Mum," Oliver said, giving it to her. "Happy Christmas. I'm sorry about…everything."

She smiled at him as she fastened it around her wrist. "Thank you," she said. Then she lowered her voice. "And the candlestick is gorgeous, too.

I would have been quite happy with that, you know." She gave him a hug and Oliver leaned against her gratefully. She believed he hadn't stolen the watch, at least. That was something.

After lunch, Thug and Thugette sloped off to try the new computer their parents had given them. Oliver was glad to see them go. Since Mr. Doorcreak had turned up, he hadn't been able to bring himself to speak to either of them. How could Oliver ever have trusted Thug with the present-swap, like that? He'd never trust him again, that was for sure.

He decided to try out the new walkie-talkie set to cheer himself up. There were two receivers, so he held one, and gave

the other to the Witch Baby to talk into.
"I'll go into the kitchen, and then we can
see if it works, okay?" he said to her.

Then he went out of the room, and
clicked his receiver on. "Hello?" he said
into the mouthpiece. "Hello? Can you
hear me?"

There was a silence. Unfortunately, the Witch Baby was toddling after her hairy spider, so she didn't reply.

Oliver was just about to turn off the speaker on his receiver, when he heard another voice.

"I think we should lock up the family silver, Merv, don't you? And my jewellery too. I don't want anything else to get stolen!"

Oliver flushed as his aunt's words

crackled through the walkie-talkie. She really thought that he was a thief! And now she was worrying that he was after her rotten old jewellery!

With shaking fingers, Oliver switched off his receiver, not wanting to hear any more. How he wished he could clear his name – and make his aunt and uncle realize who had *really* stolen the watch. It was so unfair for them to blame him!

He stuffed the walkie-talkie into his cloak pocket…and then a brilliant idea floated into his head. The sweet from the cracker was starting to work! What if…? Yes! That might just do it!

He ran to get the other walkie-talkie receiver, his mind racing. He had to make this work. He just had to!

Chapter
Six

"So, Dad, are you sure you know what to do?" Oliver asked a few moments later.

His dad nodded. "Yes," he said. "Good luck!"

Oliver took a deep breath and went upstairs, the walkie-talkie receiver still in his cloak pocket. He knocked on Thug's bedroom door, and plastered a big fake grin on his face as he went in.

"Hey, that was a good one," he said, forcing a laugh.

Thug and Thugette both had their backs to him, as they played their new computer game. At Oliver's words, Thug swung around. "What do you mean?" he asked.

"Your trick – with the watch," Oliver said. He shook his head, chuckling, as if he thought it was all a great big joke. "You totally got me there!"

Thug guffawed. "I did, didn't I?" he said smugly, leaning back in his chair. "I thought old Doorcreak was going to throttle you when he came in."

Thugette finished blasting a goblin on the computer screen, and turned around. "Your face, Oliver! I thought you were going to cry!"

Oliver gritted his teeth. His jaw muscles were starting to ache from keeping up his false grin. "I nearly did," he said. "So…when did you pinch it, then? The watch, I mean?" He crossed his fingers behind his back as he waited for

Thug's reply. He hoped they could hear all of this downstairs! He'd told his dad to make sure everyone was in the living room, where he'd set up the other walkie-talkie receiver. But Thug and Thugette didn't know *that*, of course.

"Day before you got here." Thug sniggered. "They've got a pet griffin, right? So I sneaked through the griffin-flap in the back door and had a nosey around. Couldn't resist checking out the prezzies under the Prickletree. Unwrapped a few, just to see what Old Creaky had got for his missus. And there it was, the watch. Begging to be pinched. Begging!"

"Easy as that," Thugette cackled. "My brother, the genius!"

There was a heavy tramp of footsteps coming up the stairs at that moment. And then, along the corridor came Aunt Wart, clutching the other walkie-talkie receiver, looking furious.

"Thug!" she bellowed. "I just heard all of that. I want a word with you, boy – right NOW!"

Thug's face dropped. Thugette gave a frightened gasp.

Aunt Wart swung into the room, her eyes blazing. "My own son, a thief!" she shouted. "How could you do such a thing? And letting Oliver take the blame for it, too!" She buried her face in her hands. "You've *ruined* Christmas!"

Aunt Wart ended up having quite a few words with her son and daughter. And she had one for Oliver, too – sorry.

"Thug and Thugette are going straight round to the Doorcreaks' tomorrow to apologize," she assured him. "And I'm taking their new computer away from them as a punishment." She waved her wand over it and it vanished in a puff of silver smoke. "There — I've sent it straight to your house, Oliver. My way of apologizing."

"Aw, Mu-um," Thug moaned, his bottom lip sliding out in a pout. "That's not fair."

"Oh yes it is," Aunt Wart said, folding her arms across her chest. "And you can miss your Christmas tea, and stay up here all evening, too. That's fair!"

A cloud hung over everyone for the rest of Christmas Day. Aunt Wart was in a bad mood, and Thug and Thugette stamped about upstairs.

"I knew we should have stayed at home," Oliver heard his dad muttering to his mum as they put the Witch Baby to bed that evening.

"I wish we had," Mrs. Moon replied. "Poor Oliver's had a horrible time. We'll leave first thing in the morning."

It was the only time Oliver had gone to bed with a smile on his face all week.

The next morning, though, Oliver's smile vanished as his mum opened the front door.

"Told you we'd get snowed in!" Uncle Merv chuckled. "Oh well, looks like you'll be staying a little while longer!"

Oliver couldn't help groaning at his uncle's words. For it was true – they *were* snowed in. The snow was halfway up the door frame. There was no way they were going to be able to wade out and get their broomsticks.

"The Spellicopter's blades are frozen

solid, too," Aunt Wart reported, with a shiver. "Otherwise you could have borrowed that."

"If only we'd brought our broomsticks inside," Mrs. Moon sighed, with a sideways look at her sister. "We could have flown out of one of the windows, but..."

She fell silent, gazing out at the white garden. You could just about make out the shapes of the snow-covered broomsticks, over by the shed, Oliver thought. If there was just some way of getting over there, moving the snow somehow...

Then he grinned as the second brilliant idea popped into his head. He was *so* pleased he'd eaten that sweet from the cracker! "Got it!" he laughed. "How about using the Stardust-sucker? We can suck up all the snow and clear a path to the broomsticks!"

Mr. Moon stared at him, and then out of the door at the garden. "I don't know if it would work on snow..." he said doubtfully. "But I'll give it a try." He fumbled in his pocket for the little Stardust-sucker he'd got from his cracker. "Let's have a look..."

He flicked the switch to where it said SUCK, and pointed it at the snow. The Stardust-sucker gave a mighty roar and cleared away a metre of snow in one gulp.

"Wow," Oliver marvelled. "Where did it all go?"

"According to this, it shrinks the stardust – or snow in this case – so small you can't see it," his mum said, reading the box. "And then, to empty it out, you turn the switch to RELEASE, and bingo, there's your stardust." She grinned. "Now that's magic!"

It took no time at all for Mr. Moon to make a path to the family's broomsticks. Then, once the Witch Baby was strapped in, and the Moons' cases had been magicked off home, they said their goodbyes. Things seemed rather frosty between Oliver's mum and Aunt Wart. And Uncle Merv's handshake was definitely rather limper and less

bone-crushing than it had been when they'd arrived. Thug and Thugette were still sulking upstairs, but Oliver caught sight of them at the window as he got on his broomstick. He waved at them cheerfully.

"Good riddance," he muttered under his breath, as he flew away.

It was great to get back to their house. The Prickletree was even huger than it had been when they'd left, and Oliver spent a happy hour decorating it with all the family trinkets.

His cousins' new computer was waiting for him in his bedroom, and he had a brilliant time playing all the games on it.

Later he helped his mum and dad make all his favourite Christmassy foods – chocolate frog, minced eyes, and a lovely Christmas snake.

The only thing that was missing was the snow, Oliver thought, gazing out of the window later that day. It hadn't snowed at all in Cacklewick.

And that was when he had his third brilliant idea. He went out into the garden, pointed the Stardust-sucker at the lawn, and flicked the switch to RELEASE.

"Yes!" he cheered, as the garden turned white before his eyes. "It's snowy in Cacklewick after all!"

Then he ran straight inside, grabbed the lizardphone and dialled Jake's number.

"Hi, Jake," he said. "We're back early. Fancy coming round for a snowball fight?"

The End

Oliver Moon
Junior Wizard

Collect all of Oliver Moon's magical adventures!

Oliver Moon and the Potion Commotion

Trouble is brewing when Oliver Moon is up against his arch-rival in the Young Wizard of the Year award.   ISBN 9780746073063

Oliver Moon and the Dragon Disaster

Oliver is sure he can heat things up a bit at the Festival of Magic with the help of his sister's new pet dragon. ISBN 9780746073070

Oliver Moon and the Nipperbat Nightmare

It's Oliver's turn to look after the school pet, Nippy, for the holidays. But when Nippy escapes things go horribly wrong...

ISBN 9780746077917

Oliver Moon's Summer Howliday

Oliver's summer holiday is going swimmingly until he starts to suspect there is something odd about his hairy new friend, Wilf.

ISBN 9780746077924

Oliver Moon's Christmas Cracker

Oliver is sure Christmas at his horrible Aunt Wart's is going to be dreadful, but can a very special Christmas present save the day?

ISBN 9780746077931

Oliver Moon and the Spell-off

Oliver hopes that he'll win the spell-off against clever Casper, because he can't face the scary forfeit...

ISBN 9780746077948

Oliver Moon's Fangtastic Sleepover

Oliver is on a school sleepover at a haunted house museum, but will he make it through the night when a swarm of vampire bats arrives?
Coming soon...   ISBN 9780746084793

All books are priced at £3.99